D1063714

The Bright Idea Series

LANI LARSON

First Edition

PAGE PUBLISHING, INC.
New York, NY

First originally published by Page Publishing, Inc. 2018

ISBN 978-1-64138-050-8 (Hardcover)
ISBN 978-1-64138-049-2 (Digital)

Printed in the United States of America

The Lombardi's

4

The door to apartment number 4 slowly opened, and Jack peeked his redhead through the crack. Then he hesitantly pushed it the rest of the way. After a quick glance around, Jack pushed his glasses up his nose and switched on the light stand. Mr. Watts immediately awoke!

"Hello!" Jack stumbled back a bit, and he looked across the room and up at a light stand that had come to life! Jack's jaw hung open as he saw eyes looking back at him, lightbulbs being used as hands to gesture, and a mouth moving up and down, speaking to him.

"Welcome to apartment number 4. I'm Mr. Watts," Mr. Watts bowed grandly. "I've lived here my whole life. What's your name?"

Jack stuttered back, "H-h-hi, Mr. Watts, I'm Jack." He was looking Mr. Watts up and down, glancing behind him, then said, "You're a lamp that's alive! How can that be?"

Mr. Watts smiled and said, "Well, you see, Jack, you're a kid. And kids can see magic and possibilities. Sadly, adults have lost that ability. I'm so happy you're here. Where's your family?"

Jack yet again pushed his glasses up and said, "My mom, Laura, is at the store buying our dinner for tonight." And then he mumbled, "As for the other people that will live here, they aren't my real family. My mother's husband, Anthony, and his son, Dominic, are unloading the truck." Jack sighed and said, "Mom asked that I help, so I better get going."

Mr. Watts replied, "I'm so excited to have you here! I can get pretty lonely. Are you going to be staying long, Jack?"

Jack shrugged his small shoulders and said, "Just until my mom and Anthony can find a place big enough for all of us." Then, adding in almost a whisper, he said, "Mom and I fit just fine in our old house, until she met Anthony."

"Well, just know I'm here if you ever need a friend to talk to. And please tell your brother, Dominic, the same too," Mr. Watts said with a big smile.

Jack quickly replied, "He's not my brother! Our parents just happen to be married. Not to mention we're nothing alike. I get good grades in school, and I love playing on my computer. And even though we're the same age, Dominic is so much taller and great at sports. He only struggles with schoolwork. My mom says he learns slower in certain subjects."

Mr. Watts's eyebrows drew together, and he said, "Not being able to keep up with friends can be really tough. I bet Dominic can feel very alone."

Jack's pale, freckled face seemed to redden a bit as he replied, "Dominic is the most popular kid in our classroom and even our whole school." Jack's eyes went from Mr. Watts to the floor, and he said, "Listen, I've got to go now."

Mr. Watts said goodbye and began to worry. Jack seemed very upset and kind of sad. He wanted to see Jack smile, which had Mr. Watts saying to himself, "I hope I can help Jack."

Mr. Watts found it quite wonderful seeing the apartment come to life with a family again. Laura and Anthony had time-consuming careers, where Laura was gone all day and Anthony was gone all night. Laura was a nurse at an emergency room. Mr. Watts would watch her race around the apartment early every morning. She would be moving so fast and be doing so many things at one time. Mr. Watts often thought she moved as if someone put her on fast-forward. He especially enjoyed seeing which cartoon character would be on her hospital uniform, each day. Laura's bright-blond hair was so long it would hang to the bottom of her shirt. So every single day, after she put on her sneakers, he would watch in fascination as she weaved her tiny fingers in and out to make a braid. It would hang like a long, shiny rope. He found it funny that every so often, she would stop and push her glasses up her freckled nose just the way Jack did. By the time the boys would run off the school bus in the afternoon, she would reappear again.

After dinner, Anthony would put on his police uniform and then go pat both boys' heads with a smile. Although each time, Jack would duck out of his reach. This never deterred Anthony, though. And then he would lean way down and kiss Laura on her forehead. Mr. Watts enjoyed this peaceful routine.

However, Mr. Watts began to notice Jack looking defeated when he returned home from school. After dinner, the boys would begin their homework. It was then that Mr. Watts would see Dominic become very frustrated. These observations began to worry Mr. Watts.

Finally, one weekend Laura exclaimed, "I'm going to go look at the house you saw for sale, Anthony. Will you stay here? I'll be back in a bit."

Anthony said that would be fine because he had planned to work in the kitchenette all day, making his famous chili. Dominic was at basketball practice. Once the apartment became quiet, Jack logged off his computer and strolled over to click Mr. Watts on.

Mr. Watts awoke. He smiled widely and said, "Hi, Jack! How are you?"

Jack cleared his throat, pushed his glasses up his nose, and said, "Um, well, you said that I could talk to you any time. And I felt I needed a friend."

"Of course, Jack, that's what friends are for. What's on your mind?" Mr. Watts replied.

"Well, I just wish that I was part of a real family. It's not fair. My friends at school have sisters and brothers that they are actually related to!"

Mr. Watts pondered this, and he said, "Jack, when you come home from school, you seem very upset. What happens there to make you feel that way?"

Jack looked down and said, "The boys in my gym class make fun of me, because I'm smaller and not good at sports."

4

Mr. Watts asks, “Then what happens? I’ve never heard your mom being called to the school for a fight?”

Jack says, “Because Dominic stands in front of me and tells them to leave me alone.”

Mr. Watts smiles triumphantly, “Jack, you need to understand something. A family is made in many different ways. Like loyalty and standing up for each other. And the way Dominic protected you from those bullies was the act of a brother.”

Jack was trying his best to hold back tears as he said, “You’re right, Mr. Watts! Dominic is my brother. What can I do to show him that I think of him as my brother, the way he does for me?”

Mr. Watts smiled and asked, “Jack, do you deep in your heart have faith in your family—faith that they love you and you can always depend on them?”

Without missing a beat, Jack nodded, “Of course, Mr. Watts.”

“Then I have a bright idea,” countered Mr. Watts. It was at this exact moment that all of his lightbulbs brightened beautifully and the whole room became illuminated by them.

Jack’s eyes widened, and he felt a sense of hope wash over him.

"I think the answer to your question is in returning the favor to Dominic. By Dominic standing up for you, that was his way of showing he cares. Being athletic and outgoing are his strengths. Jack, what are your strengths that you could share with Dominic?"

Jack straightened proudly and said, "I am a really good student, and schoolwork is easy for me. Plus, I excel on the computer."

"So, Jack, just as Dominic shared his naturally given gifts with you, maybe you could do the same. You have said that he struggles with his schoolwork," Mr. Watts replied.

Jack answered with a huge smile, "That's it! Thank you, Mr. Watts. I will ask Dominic tonight if he wants to do our homework together."

That evening, when everyone was eating Anthony's delicious chili, Jack asked, "Hey, Dominic, I was wondering if you'd want to do our homework together tonight. I know we have that big math test coming up soon, and I can show you some tricks I learned to help with our multiplication tables. It's pretty cool. And maybe after, I could show you a video game I'm inventing. I'm kind of stuck. Maybe you could help me with it?"

Dominic's dark-brown eyes lit up, and he turned his ball cap backward as he readily agreed. Then he turned to Laura and Anthony and asked, "Can we get a ride to the park tomorrow so I can give Jack some pointers on the basketball court?"

Jack's eyes widened as he added, "Please! Can we? Dominic knows how to make almost every shot—although I'm probably too short to ever be any good." Jack was looking down at his dinner plate at this point.

Dominic quickly replied, "That's not true! Some great basketball players are smaller. And they are some of the fastest players on the court, Jack."

Jack sat up straighter, smiled, and repeated, "Well, can we get a ride tomorrow to the park and stay long enough for Dominic to show me how to shoot?"

Mr. Watts saw Anthony reach over to hold Laura's hand and reply, "I think we could manage that."

After everyone got up from the table, Mr. Watts noticed for the first time that Jack didn't duck when Anthony went to tussle his hair.

A couple weeks later, Mr. Watts watched the Lombardi's fill up their truck with all their boxes and belongings. The house that Anthony had told Laura about was just what she had envisioned. Two days later, Anthony received a call from the bank, and the house was sold to them. During these past two weeks, Mr. Watts had so enjoyed watching the boys transform from just classmates and roommates to brothers.

Anthony was always repeating, "Laura, our boys are thick as thieves."

On this day of packing and making trips to the new house, Dominic and Jack had to be reminded, a few times, to get off the computer, put the basketball down, and to quit goofing around. They would then break into fits of laughter and begin to carry boxes outside.

Mr. Watts saw Laura give the apartment one last look, and then she turned to leave. Right before she closed the door, Jack ran past her and said he would be right out. Jack, for the last time, turned and switched Mr. Watts on.

BOOKS
VACUUM
SPORTS EQUIPMENT
MICROWAVE

With a sweaty face, and his glasses halfway off his nose, Jack said, "Mr. Watts, I'm going to miss you. Are you going to be okay here alone?"

Mr. Watts smiled and replied, "Thank you for your concern, friend. But all is well. I heard the manager say there will be a new family moving in next week. I know there will be more adventures to come."

Jack pushed his glasses up and replied, "Mr. Watts, thank you for helping me to see that the true meaning of family is much more than being related."

Mr. Watts said, "You're very welcome, Jack. But I just gave you a bright idea. Your love for your family took you the rest of the way."

Jack turned and clicked the switch off to Mr. Watts. "Goodbye, Mr. Watts, I'll remember you forever."

And Mr. Watts thought the Lombardi family would be just fine. As the door closed, Mr. Watts wondered about the future family to live in apartment number 4 and what bright ideas were yet to come …

Hi, my name is:
And my *Bright Idea* for today is:

The Leonard's

4

The door to apartment number 4 swung open so hard it hit the wall with a bang. With a big sigh, Bridgette clicked on the switch to the light stand so she could assess where she would be living for now.

"Hello!" Bridgette inhaled quickly and put her hand to her heart. Then realizing she lost her composure, she smoothed out her purple shirt and flicked her golden hair behind her shoulder. Her blue eyes traveled all the way up the light stand that had somehow come to life. In disbelief, she saw eyes looking down at her, lips that were smiling, and lightbulbs that were being used to gesture.

"Welcome to apartment number 4. I'm Mr. Watts," he said as he bowed grandly. "I've lived here my whole life. What's your name?"

Bridgette crossed her long arms in front of her, stuck her right leg out defiantly, and said, "I'm Bridgette. And I would like to know, just what exactly is going on here? How am I speaking with a light stand?"

Mr. Watts smiled, seemingly undeterred from Bridgette's tough demeanor, said, "Well, you see, Bridgette, you're a kid. And kids can see magic and possibilities, whereas adults have lost that ability. I'm so happy you're here. Where's your family?"

With her arms still crossed, she reluctantly answered, "My grandparents are getting my twin brothers out of their car seats. They are three-year-old terrors!" Bridgette rolled her eyes at that last comment.

Mr. Watts watched her go from defiant to a bit sad as she cleared her throat and said, "My parents are in a different country right now." After a beat, she straightened herself yet again and said, "I should begin cleaning and putting our belongings in their proper place. There is so much to do."

"I'm so excited to have you here! I can get pretty lonely when there's no family living here. Are you going to stay long, Bridgette?" Mr. Watts asked enthusiastically.

Bridgette glanced down for a second before replying, "Just until my parents finish building two houses for Habitat for Humanity. They volunteer about four times a year." By this point, Bridgette was staring out the window, lost in her thoughts.

Mr. Watts replied, "Habitat for Humanity is a lovely charity! Helping families that are in need of a home. You must be so proud of them!"

Bridgette snapped her head up to Mr. Watts, flicked her hair behind her shoulder, and replied, "Yeah, I'm really happy that *my* parents can help *others*! Listen, I've got to get to work."

"Okay, Bridgette, just remember, I'm here if you ever need anything." Mr. Watts barely got out those words before Bridgette was gone, slamming the door behind her.

Mr. Watts thought Bridgette seemed angry, sad, and much too serious. He realized he didn't see her smile once.

Mr. Watts thought to himself, *I hope I can help Bridgette.*

Mr. Watts watched gleefully as the apartment came to life again with the Leonard family. Tom and Mary seemed like young grandparents, having no trouble keeping up with the twins, Emmett and Mickey. They were identical, both with light-brown hair that seemed to curl at the bottom. Mr. Watts found it funny how they did everything with such energy and excitement. It showed when they were playing with their toys or wrestling each other, but it even showed when they ate. The boys appeared to not take a breath from one bite to the next. Then each of them giggled in delight at the mess they had created. When it was time for their naps, Tom would rock them back and forth to the sound of his rumbling voice as he hummed lullabies. At this point, Mickey always had a piece of Tom's snow-white hair locked in his fist. Once asleep, there was no noise or commotion that could stir them awake. The twins appeared to live in constant joy.

Mr. Watts loved how Mary's smile seemed to bring peace to anyone she came into contact with. He wondered if she was aware of her power. And her hair was like a color Mr. Watts had never seen. The same strands of gold as Bridgette's, but with bright white mixed in around her face, making Mary appear almost angelic. And then there was Tom's laugh. Mr. Watts thought this apartment could be empty, but with just Tom's laugh, it would still feel like a home. Tom believed that laughter was an emotion that should be felt and shown always. He wondered why some people tried to stifle one of the great joys of life. Yet amongst the fun, Mr. Watts couldn't help but notice that Bridgette still appeared lonely and so serious.

Mr. Watts would watch Bridgette struggle with her math homework each evening after dinner. Her usually big, blue eyes would become small as she squinted in frustration. Mary knew her granddaughter well, and when that squint appeared, she knew

Bridgette was becoming irritated. Once Mary saw that clue, she would come to Bridgette's aide instantly, knowing how difficult it was for Bridgette to ask for help. Once Mary intervened, Mr. Watts would see Bridgette's face relax with relief. However, he felt that her math struggles weren't the only thing bothering her.

One nice spring day, Mary exclaimed, "Tom, these boys have been cooped up inside this apartment too long. I'm taking them to the park."

She realized she would not get a reply, as she heard Tom snoring in their bedroom. Mary and the boys giggled. Tom's snoring was louder than a grizzly bear's roar. Once alone, because she didn't feel like going to the park too, Bridgette strolled into the living room.

She glanced up at Mr. Watts, and after waiting a couple of beats, she clicked the switch that made him come alive. Bridgette, not wanting her awe to show, kept her face neutral.

Mr. Watts awakened and said, "Hi, Bridgette! It's been awhile since we've spoken. How is everything?"

Bridgette shrugged her small shoulder, and right before she was about to answer him, something seemed to switch in her mind, and she swung her golden hair over her shoulder and stated, "I'm fine. Everything is just fine."

Mr. Watt's eyebrows rose as he said, "Bridgette, I consider you a friend. And it's okay to share with friends, especially when something is bothering you. This doesn't make you weak. It's actually quite courageous to share your feelings!" He watched her ponder that statement for a couple of seconds, and then she nodded her head, as if she had made up her mind.

"Mr. Watts, I just really miss my mom and dad. I don't think it's fair that my friends live with their parents while my brothers and I have to stay with our grandparents most of the year."

Mr. Watts felt for Bridgette as he replied, "Missing people you love can be a very difficult feeling. I'm sorry you are struggling, Bridgette. But it's very important to remember why your parents aren't here right now. They are helping people in need."

Bridgette nodded and then stuck her foot out a bit defiantly, "I know. But why do they have to help so much?"

Mr. Watts could see Bridgette becoming irritated with his answers, so he further explained, "Bridgette, helping others is a wonderful gift. Because when you help someone, not only does it improve their lives but it makes you feel good too. Then Mr. Watts asked, “Bridgette, you struggle with your math homework, right?”

She folded her arms in front of her, stuck her chin up a bit, and replied, “Yeah, so what?”

Mr. Watts continued, “What happens, Bridgette, when you get stuck on a math problem?”

Bridgette’s eyes slowly widened as she answered, “Right away, Gram is at my side.”

Mr. Watts smiled and said, “That’s right, Bridgette. And when I watch Mary help you, I see the relief on your face and the pleasure on hers. It can be such a wonderful feeling to help others!”

What had started out as a small lifting of her mouth had spread into a big, bright smile—a smile Mr. Watts had never seen. He loved that her smile was so similar to Mary’s.

Bridgette slowly let her arms fall to her sides as she said, “Mr. Watts, I have been so selfish. How can I show my grandparents how grateful I am for all they do?”

Mr. Watts smiled and asked, “Bridgette, do you deep in your heart have faith in your family—faith that they love you and you can always depend on them?”

Without missing a beat, Bridgette nodded, "Of course, Mr. Watts."

"Then I have a bright idea," countered Mr. Watts.

It was at this exact moment that all his lightbulbs brightened so beautifully, and the whole room became illuminated by them.

Bridgette's eyes widened, and she felt a sense of hope wash over her.

"Your brothers are very young and full of energy. You could help by playing with them more. That would lift your grandparents' burden and free up extra time for them. This will also relieve your parents concern every time they leave, because they will know you are becoming a very helpful member of the family."

And just like usual, Bridgette threw her shiny hair behind her shoulder, smiled, and said, "Thank you, Mr. Watts! I can't wait to get started."

That evening Mr. Watts watched the Leonard's have dinner. He felt pure joy as he watched Bridgette settle Emmett and Mickey at the table. She poured their drinks, wiped their messy mouths, and cleaned up their plates after inhaling their food. Just when Mr.

Watts thought he couldn't feel any happier, he saw Mary and Tom exchange relieved smiles at Bridgette's new helpfulness.

Mr. Watts had really enjoyed watching Bridgette play with Emmett and Mickey these past weeks. It even allowed for Mary and Tom to work on their own activities. Mr. Watts's favorite change, however, was Bridgette. She had decided to volunteer twice a week, after school, tutoring classmates in Spanish. This was her best subject.

The day before Bridgette began tutoring, she told Mary she would be home late the next day, and Mary asked how come.

Bridgette smiled and said, "Gram, math comes so easy to you. And even though you have so many other things to do, you always make time to help me. It made me wonder how I could help someone just like you do. I thought how I've been speaking Spanish for two years now, which means I could tutor kids just beginning. I really understand how frustrating it can be when you cannot understand a subject."

Mary's cheeks pinked with pleasure as she replied, "I'm so proud of you, Bridgette! Helping others and volunteering is one of the great ways to make this world a better place." Then Mary

added, "It's great to see you take after your parents. They started volunteering after they had received help."

This really caught Bridgette's attention as she replied, "Gram, what exactly do you mean?"

Mary seemed to think for a second and then decided to share, "Bridgette, your parents didn't have much money when they were just married. They didn't even have full-time work yet, and paying their rent was becoming impossible. So Grandpa and I gave them money. Not knowing if they would have a place to live was a feeling they couldn't forget. Eventually, building houses for those in need was an easy decision."

Bridgette was in more awe of her family than ever. A few weeks passed, and Mr. Watts was now watching the commotion of the Leonard's packing up to move out of apartment number 4. Two weeks earlier, Bridgette's parents had returned, with a big surprise. While they were on their last trip, they had arranged for a new house to be built. It was a regular house, but with an extra bedroom, bathroom, kitchenette, and living area. This made for plenty of room for Mary and Tom. Now Bridgette and her brothers would not have to move every time their parents went on a mission for Habitat for Humanity.

Once everyone was settled in their big SUV with the twins secure in their car seats, Bridgette ran back inside one last time. She reached for the switch that turned on Mr. Watts.

Bridgette tucked her hair behind her ear and said, "Mr. Watts, I'm going to miss you. Are you going to be okay here alone?"

Mr. Watts smiled and replied, "Thank you for your concern, friend. But all is well. I heard the manager say there will be a new family moving in next week. I know there will be more adventures to come."

Bridgette stood relaxed and happy, so different from when she had first moved in. She said, "Mr. Watts, thank you for teaching me how wonderful helping others can be."

Mr. Watts said, "You're very welcome, Bridgette. But I just gave you a bright idea. Your love for your family took you the rest of the way."

Bridgette clicked off the switch to Mr. Watts for the last time and said, "Goodbye, Mr. Watts, I'll remember you forever."

And Mr. Watts thought the Leonard family would be just fine. As the door closed, Mr. Watts wondered about the future family to live in apartment number 4 and what bright ideas were yet to come.

Hi, my name is:
And my *Bright Idea* for today is:

The Quinn's

4

The door to apartment number 4 was pushed open by Liam as he dropped two bags full of clothes. He was not paying attention to what he was doing because he was too busy bopping his head to the music coming out of his earbuds. He swiped his messy black hair away from his eyes and realized it was dark, so he turned to his right, and flicked the switch to the light stand.

Mr. Watts awakened immediately!

"Hello!"

Liam thought he heard something, so he pulled one earbud out and said, "Who's there?"

But as he scanned the apartment, his eyes turned and his head tilted all the way up to the tall light stand in front of the window. And to his amazement, he saw the light stand had come to life! It was looking at him, smiling and gesturing with his lightbulbs as if they were hands!

"Welcome to apartment number 4. I'm Mr. Watts," he bowed grandly. "I've lived here my whole life. What's your name?"

Liam shuffled his feet hesitantly, quickly pulled the other earbud out, and with building excitement, said, "Uh, hey, I'm Liam Quinn."

As he was saying this, his big, brown eyes were opened wide in awe of the sight before him. Instantly, he said, "Wow, wait until my parents see you!"

Mr. Watts replied, "I'm sorry, Liam, but they will only see a light stand. They will not see what you see."

Liam's excited face seemed to dim somewhat. "Why? I don't understand …"

Mr. Watts explained, "Adults lose their ability to see magic. Being a kid is a very special time. Your mind is open to all possibilities and ideas."

Liam seemed to regain some of his enthusiasm as he asked, "Well, can you be my friend while I live here?"

Mr. Watts smiled widely and says, "I would like that very much, Liam. And I can't wait to see the rest of your family. Are they coming?"

Liam nodded his head and replied, "I have to help my parents bring in all our stuff. My dad can do some things, but he's in a wheelchair. He was a soldier and lost his leg in a war. But he does supercool things with his wheelchair, and he's even in a basketball club with other guys in wheelchairs." Liam seemed to run out of steam as he said, "And you'll see my little sister, Abby. She is only four." Liam rolled his eyes and shrugged his small shoulders. "She can only carry in baby things. My mom has to do almost everything for her."

Mr. Watts smiles in understanding. "I'm very excited to have your family live here! Do you know how long you will be staying?"

Liam fidgeted with his red T-shirt and says, "No, I'm not sure. We just moved to this town, and we're waiting for our new house to be built. The lady who's in charge said it would take longer than usual. It needs to be able to fit my dad's wheelchair. In our old house, he would get stuck in doorways."

Liam glanced down and then looked back up at Mr. Watts and said wishfully, "I hope we can be friends because my family is always so busy."

Mr. Watts had a big smile as he replied, "I would like that very much. And I can also be friends with your little sister, Abby."

Mr. Watts saw Liam's eyes rolled again then looked at his partially tied shoelaces and squirmed a bit and said, "Yeah, I'm sure. She *always* has to do everything I do. Plus, she gets all the attention because she's smaller." Then he stood straighter and said, "Well, I guess I better run back out and finish unpacking."

Mr. Watts replied, "Okay, Liam. I'm really happy you and your family live here now. Always remember, I'm here if you need any help."

After Liam left, Mr. Watts wondered about the family that was moving in. He was so excited to meet Liam's sister, Abby, and his parents, Danny and Colleen. However, Mr. Watts couldn't escape the feeling that Liam seemed a bit sad. This had Mr. Watts feeling a bit worried and declaring, "I hope I can help Liam feel happier."

Mr. Watts watched his empty, dusty, lonely apartment come to life with flowers, furniture, and wonderful aromas from the kitchenette. Most importantly, however, were the voices, laughter, and the love of a family. The apartment transformed from just a place to live, to a real home.

Colleen had bouncy, curly hair, the color of the pumpkins Mr. Watts saw during Halloween. He didn't see Colleen sit often, though. She was usually chasing after Abby or driving everyone to one place or another. Then by night, Mr. Watts mostly saw her standing behind Liam, helping him with his homework.

Even though Danny was always sitting, it seemed to Mr. Watts as if that wheelchair was never sitting in one place for too long. Danny had to go to a place three times a week, called physical therapy. It was a place that was supposed to help him become stronger and ease some of the pain from his war injury—although Mr. Watts knew Danny didn't need stronger arms. They were extremely big from rolling his chair around every day. When Danny wasn't at physical therapy, he was checking on the progress of their new house.

The rest of Danny's time, outside the apartment, was spent at his job. Liam had told Mr. Watts that Danny worked at a place called Pets and Vets, where he placed specially trained dogs with men and women who came home from the war and were in need of extra help. At the end of Danny's long days, Mr. Watts usually saw him in the kitchenette, making dinner with Colleen. He liked the way Danny's black mustache twitched every time Colleen made a joke. Danny also made time each day to put Abby on his lap and zip her around the living room. That was Mr. Watts's favorite time of the day, watching Abby's long, auburn hair fly around her chubby pink cheeks as she laughed and laughed. However, it was also during this time that Mr. Watts would notice Liam appearing sad.

One Saturday afternoon, the Quinn's came home, and they all separated to do something different. Mr. Watts watched Danny go prepare dinner, and Colleen went to play with Abby in her bedroom. It was then that Liam walked over and switched Mr. Watts on.

Mr. Watts awakened and said, "Liam, hi, buddy! How is everything?"

And just like on the first day, Liam looked down and shuffled his feet. Then he looked up at Mr. Watts and, almost in a whisper, said, "I wish my family spent more time together. It seems like everyone always has something separate to do. And if there's any time leftover, it's for Abby."

Mr. Watts nodded and said, "Well, Abby is still very young and needs more help than you. Not to mention both your parents have a lot going on right now. Having a new house built can be very time consuming, especially when your dad needs to make sure the house can accommodate his wheelchair."

Liam nodded slowly in agreement and replied, "Yeah, I know. But I wish there was something that we could all do together," then he added, "even my sister too."

Mr. Watts understood. He asked, "Liam, do you, deep in your heart, have faith in your family—faith that they love you and you can always depend on them?"

Without missing a beat, Liam nodded, "Of course, Mr. Watts."

"Then I have a bright idea," countered Mr. Watts. It was at this exact point that all his lightbulbs brightened so beautifully, and the room became illuminated by them.

Liam's eyes widened, and he felt a sense of hope wash over him.

Mr. Watts said, "I believe the answer to your wish lies in your dad's job."

Liam looked up quizzically and replied, "But he places dogs with vets. How will that help us spend time together?"

Mr. Watts asked, "Liam, what is your father?"

Liam shuffled his feet and looked around, trying to think of an answer. Finding none, he said, "Um, he's my dad, my mom's husband, a basketball player … umm, what else?"

Mr. Watts smiled and replied, "Liam, your dad is a vet too."

4

Liam nodded and said, "Yeah, I know. He was a great soldier who got hurt in the war."

Mr. Watts continued, "What if you and your family adopt one of the dogs from Pets and Vets? Dogs are beautiful, loyal animals. And a dog would be something you would all have to work on together—teaching obedience, going on walks, having playtime, and most importantly, loving them. A dog can help people in so many ways. In fact, most animals do. But dogs are very special. Your dad knows this, Liam. This is why he arranges for them to help his fellow military comrades."

The excitement and energy that Mr. Watts saw on Liam the first day they met was back as Liam exclaimed, "That's it! Thank you, Mr. Watts. I will ask my parents at dinner tonight."

That evening Mr. Watts watched, from the living room, the Quinn's having dinner. Liam, being Liam, was very excited to present his idea. So once all the plates were filled, Colleen looked at her son and asked what had him so excited that he could barely sit. Liam took a sip of his milk and then presented his wish to the family. Mr. Watts watched Colleen and Danny lock eyes, after Liam was done speaking. Then Colleen gave such a small nod to

VETS

Danny that Mr. Watts thought he might have imagined it. Liam at this point was staring at his dinner plate, afraid to see his parents say no. Abby was blissfully unaware of what was happening. She was too busy playing with the peas on her plate.

Finally, Danny said, "Liam, look at me please."

Liam put his fork down and looked up, "Yeah, Dad?"

Danny smiled, "Son, I think that is a great idea! A dog would be a great addition to this family. How about tomorrow you come with me to work and help to pick out our dog?"

Liam's brown eyes widened. He turned his head to look at his mom and then back to his dad again as he replied, "Really? Just me, Dad?"

Danny reached over and put his hand on Liam's shoulder as he answered, "I know your mom and I have been pretty busy lately. However, this doesn't mean that we miss seeing you play patiently with your sister or how hard you're working in school. Your mom and I have complete faith that you'll find a great match for this family."

Liam jumped out of his seat, throwing his arms up, yelling, "Wahoo, we're getting a dog!"

VETS
PETS

This commotion finally caught Abby's attention. Her green eyes widened, and she squealed, "Doggie! Yay! I can be a doggie." And she began to make barking noises.

All the Quinn's began laughing. They spent the rest of the meal debating breeds and names. Mr. Watts watched happily.

About two weeks later, Mr. Watts observed the Quinn family repack all their belongings and make trip after trip from the apartment to their van. Colleen had come home two days ago, proclaiming the new house was finally ready. As each family member came in and out with boxes, that sweet little dog—named Socks—would follow each time, seeming to think it was a fun, new game to play.

Mr. Watts had heard Danny tell Colleen that he was a mix of many breeds.

Danny then said, "Socks is a true mutt."

Socks was black all over, with patches of white on his chest and belly. Mr. Watts loved how his paws were white. Against the rest of his black fur, it made it appear as if he was wearing two pairs of socks. However, it was Socks's disposition that made him a great dog. He seemed to always have his tongue hanging out, his lips pulled back, as if he was continually smiling. He never seemed upset. He would sit patiently as Abby put a tiara on his head every time she wanted to play "tea party." And Socks seemed to always know what amount of energy to use when Liam wanted to wrestle. Danny was right; Liam chose the best dog for the Quinn family.

Socks accomplished what Liam wanted. When the Quinn's were home, they were usually all in the living room together, playing and laughing at Socks's tricks and silly faces. And now when the Quinn family went to the park, they went together. A dog truly is a special animal.

Once everyone was packed into the van, with the remaining boxes, Liam came back in one last time.

Liam switched the light to Mr. Watts on. "Mr. Watts, I'm going to miss you. Are you going to be okay here alone?"

Mr. Watts smiled and replied, "Thank you for your concern, friend. But all is well. I heard the manager say there will be a new family moving in next week. I know there will be more adventures to come."

Liam smiled with his usual enthusiasm and replied, "Mr. Watts, thank you for helping us become a closer family."

Mr. Watts said, "You're very welcome, Liam. But I just gave you a bright idea. Your love for your family took you the rest of the way."

Liam turned and clicked the switch off to Mr. Watts, "Goodbye, Mr. Watts, I'll remember you forever."

And Mr. Watts thought the Quinn family would be just fine. As the door closed, Mr. Watts wondered about the future family to live in apartment number 4 and what bright ideas were yet to come …

Hi, my name is:

And my *Bright Idea* for today is:

About the Author

Lani Larson is a new author, who finds joy in writing fun yet thoughtful stories for children. Lani has earned her bachelor's degree in Psychology with a minor in Sociology from a private Upstate New York college. She has lived in the Town of Bethlehem, New York, her whole life. She lives with her wonderful husband of eleven years. Both he and her extended family have been a great support with Lani's writing endeavors. In her spare time, Lani is a devout fan of the St. Louis Cardinals, finds her Irish heritage fascinating, loves spending time with all breeds of dogs, and enjoys playing pool and going to the beach with her family. Last but not least, her guilty pleasures are reality TV shows and posting original quotes to her Facebook page.

CPSIA information can be obtained
at www.ICGtesting.com
Printed in the USA
BVHW01*2142110618
518773BV00002B/4/P

9 781641 380508